# Laura

*for Anne-Marie*

© 1976, l'école des loisirs, Paris
First published in France as
Laura, le terre-neuve d'Alice
ISBN 0 575 02568 9
Printed in Belgium ☒

# Philippe Dumas

# Laura
*Alice's New Puppy*

LONDON
VICTOR GOLLANCZ LTD
1979

If Alice's grandmother hadn't given
her a little dog that could swim
as a birthday present, the story
that you are about to hear might
have ended very differently.

It was soft and round, a furry black ball.
Alice and her brother Emil loved it.

They couldn't stop cuddling the puppy,
but even on its very first day the
poor little thing was very patient.
Alice's grandmother warned them that
her present would get bigger as it
was a Newfoundland dog.

The little dog slept next to Alice's bed.
In the middle of the night the puppy
cried a bit, but Alice spoke gently
to her and she went back to sleep.

Alice thought of a name for her.
It was such a pretty name—Laura.
The sort of name you might give a doll.
Laura was very fond of dolls!

She had three meals a day: eggs
in the morning, meat at midday
and vegetables at night.

It was soon clear that this diet
agreed with Laura because day by
day she was getting bigger.

She grew—and it was easy to see
what she preferred to eat.

She grew—and ran around madly,
bounding through flower beds
and leaping over hedges.

She felt completely at home and
she made her presence felt. She
grew—and when she played with
the children now, she always won.

Because she had grown so quickly, she forgot that she was too big for some games. Laura became a real problem. The children's mother said, "She's a menace in the house."

Laura was very friendly and
insisted on saying hello to
everybody who came to
the house.

Some people were frightened of her.

The postman put his letters into
their box very quickly.

Their neighbour no longer spoke to them.

But the butcher was friendly because
Laura was one of his best customers.

She became very strong. When she
was in the car, nothing could stop
her from sitting with the children.

In the evening, while she slept, everyone
forgave her for the day's misdeeds. But
in the morning, she was the first to get up
and the complaints started all over again.

So that's how things were until one
fateful day when Laura was left all
alone in the house.
Alice and Emil had been invited to
spend the day at their Aunt Odile's
house. Their cousins Eve, Laurie and
Biba were waiting for them so that
they could all go to the beach.

They built a huge sandcastle.
It was a perfect day.
Instead of going home
to tea with the others
Alice and Emil stayed
behind on the beach.

They borrowed Biba's rubber boat
so that they could get close to
the people who were fishing.

They didn't realise that the wind
had changed direction and that
they were being blown towards
the open sea.

On the beach, nobody saw what had
happened. Anyway, it was getting
late and all the bathers were
packing up to go home.

Aunt Odile thought that Alice and Emil had gone straight home, while their mother thought they were still with Aunt Odile. Besides, at home there were other things to worry about: Laura had been naughty again.

Was it her fault that no one had
remembered to take her for a walk
last night?

Mum said she'd had enough of Laura's tricks and it was time she was put in a kennel outside. Dad said he would start to make one the very next day.

The children didn't come back and
their father decided to fetch them
from Aunt Odile's house.

The minute he opened the door, Laura
shot past him and bounded away. "I'll
never catch up with her now," thought
Dad.

To his surprise, the children were not
at Aunt Odile's. "I thought they were
at home," she said. Everyone began to
get worried. There was nobody in the
garden.

Nobody on the beach either.

Uncle John telephones the police
and tells the whole village.
Everyone searches high and low,
but there's nobody in the woods.

There's nobody at the farm where the
children often go and play.
"They're going to search the moor
between St Aubin and Englesville,"
say the policemen.

While all this is going on, Laura tears
across the fields towards the beach.

She runs along the shore,
ignoring the waves.

Suddenly, she thinks she
can smell something.

She plunges into the cold water
and swims out into the open sea.
She gets along quickly with her
webbed feet.

Poor Emil! Poor Alice! The waves are huge and the sea is rough. They are very frightened and they huddle together on the bottom of the boat.

Emil is the first to notice Laura's
eyes glinting in the darkness.

Laura takes the tow rope in her
mouth and tries to pull the boat
along, but it's difficult. The sea
is getting wilder and wilder.

Laura battles with all her strength
against the waves and the current.

An enormous wave hurls Emil from
the boat.

Laura drops the tow rope and
dives down into the sea.

Alice is left alone. She is so
frightened that she doesn't
even cry.

Laura has fished Emil
from under the water
and pulls him to the
boat by his arm.

Alice helps him back into the boat
while Laura steadies it with her mouth.

But Laura's teeth puncture the rubber
boat and it starts to deflate.

They must abandon ship! Alice and
Emil hold tight to Laura's neck as
she struggles towards the shore, but
she begins to feel very tired.

Lightning flashes in the sky. The
sea rages. Thank goodness the beach
isn't too far away now.

At last Laura's feet touch the ground
and they're standing on dry land again.

Laura keeps the children warm by rubbing herself against them. Then she howls as loudly as she can.

The searchers have heard the howling.
They come running, carrying blankets.
Thanks to Laura, the children
have been saved.

There's no question of shutting up
Laura now. She's going to be allowed
to follow the children wherever she
wants to. To thank her, Alice and
Emil choose the biggest bone in the
butcher's shop. The mayor has sent
her a medal—for life-saving.